This Walker book belongs to:

_____

_____

_____

First published 1986 by Walker Books Ltd
87 Vauxhall Walk, London SE11 5HJ

This edition published 2015

2 4 6 8 10 9 7 5 3 1

The right of Colin West to be identified as author/illustrator of this work
has been asserted by him in accordance with the Copyright, Designs and Patents Act 1988

This book has been typeset in Optima

Printed in China

British Library Cataloguing in Publication Data:
a catalogue record for this book is available from the British Library

ISBN 978-1-4063-6752-2

www.walker.co.uk

"Pardon?" said the giraffe

Colin West

WALKER BOOKS
AND SUBSIDIARIES
LONDON • BOSTON • SYDNEY • AUCKLAND

"What's it like up there?"
asked the frog
as he hopped on the ground.

"Pardon?"
said the
giraffe.

"What's it like up there?"
asked the frog
as he hopped on the lion.

"Pardon?"
said the
giraffe.

"What's it like up there?"
asked the frog
as he hopped on the hippo.

"Pardon?"
said the
giraffe.

"What's it like up there?"
asked the frog
as he hopped on the elephant.

"Pardon?"
said the
giraffe.

"What's it like up there?"
asked the frog
as he hopped on the giraffe.

"It's nice up here, thank you,"
said the giraffe,
"but you're tickling my nose
and I think I'm going to..."

A-A-A-TISHOOOOO

Colin West says that the idea for *"Pardon?" said the Giraffe*
came to him because he wanted to write a story
about animals of different heights.
He says, "A giraffe is the natural choice for a tall animal,
while a frog provided me with a good, cheeky, small character.
'What's it like up there?' is a phrase rather tall people often
have to put up with. In my story I think the giraffe can
hear the question perfectly well, but she is determined to
wear out the rude frog as he hops higher and higher."